The Naughty List

The Naughty List

Alain M. Bergeron

illustrated by
Sampar

translated by
Marie-Michèle Gingras

Scholastic Canada Ltd.
Toronto New York London Auckland Sydney
Mexico City New Delhi Hong Kong Buenos Aires

Scholastic Canada Ltd.
604 King Street West, Toronto, Ontario M5V 1E1, Canada

Scholastic Inc.
557 Broadway, New York, NY 10012, USA

Scholastic Australia Pty Limited
PO Box 579, Gosford, NSW 2250, Australia

Scholastic New Zealand Limited
Private Bag 94407, Botany, Manukau 2163, New Zealand

Scholastic Children's Books
Euston House, 24 Eversholt Street, London NW1 1DB, UK

Library and Archives Canada Cataloguing in Publication
Bergeron, Alain M., 1957-
[Ma sœur n'est pas un cadeau!. English]
The naughty list / by Alain M. Bergeron ; illustrations
by Sampar ; translation by Marie-Michèle Gingras.
Translation of: Ma sœur n'est pas un cadeau!.
ISBN 978-1-4431-1394-6
I. Sampar II. Gingras, Marie-Michèle III. Title.
IV. Title: Ma sœur n'est pas un cadeau! English.
PS8553.E67454M313 2012   C843'.54   C2012-901650-0

6 5 4 3 2 1   Printed in Canada 121   12 13 14 15 16

To Marie-Michèle Gingras, without whom this book would not have been made.
— A.M.B.

Chapter 1
Bad Idea!

This wasn't a good idea. Not at all.

My sister Isabelle and I are walking to the mall. So far one of her boots has fallen off five times!

The first time it happened, I felt sorry for her. It's freezing outside and her foot is so tiny. She had to stand on one leg in the snow.

She looked like a flamingo in a snowsuit!

The second time it happened, she hid her foot up in her snowpants. Then she stuck it out and in again.

"Peek-a-boo, Dominic!" she said, giggling at her silliness.

My sister is so childish sometimes!

Now her boot has just come off for the fifth time. She's still giggling, but my sympathy is gone. It's too cold out for this!

I put her boot back on and stand up. "Isabelle, enough! Your toes could freeze and fall off. Do you know what that means?"

"That I can put them under my pillow for the Toe Fairy?" she says.

I blink. "The who?"

"The Toe Fairy! She's the Tooth Fairy's cousin," Isabelle explains.

"What? No! It means you will need new boots. Because without any toes, your old boots will be too big!"

"But if the Toe Fairy gives me a dollar for each toe, I'll have enough money to buy new boots," says Isabelle.

She can be pretty smart for a little kid.

"Come on," I say. "We have to find gifts for Grandpa and Grandma. Santa only comes for kids. It's up to us to find something nice for them."

"Yes!" she cheers. "Let's go!" She starts to hop, swinging her arms and her legs.

And her boot falls off for the sixth time.

Chapter 2
With a Little Help From My Friends

We are at the mall at last! It feels so good to be inside.

As we warm up, I go through my list of *Dos and Don'ts* with Isabelle.

"If you get lost, you sit right where you are. Stay there and I'll find you. Got it?"

"Got it," she says. "Hey, speaking of sitting

down, do you know where the washrooms are? I really have to go."

Uh-oh. How did I get myself into this? I'm not going into the women's washroom! And I cannot — and will not — bring her with me into the men's room. She will just have to go by herself.

"But who's going to help me when I'm done?" Isabelle asks in her little voice. Her eyes are big. She's trying to charm me.

"Don't use that voice with me! That only works on Dad," I tell her. "You always say you're a big girl. Here's your chance to prove it. I'll wait outside."

My sister walks into the washroom.

Five long minutes later, she comes out. She looks proud of herself. And, somehow, a little more grown-up. But as she gets closer, I notice a long strip of toilet paper hanging from the back of her pants.

My sister is so embarrassing sometimes!

"Isabelle, what's that?" I ask. "What are you doing?"

She turns around.

"Ooooh!" she shouts, looking pleased. "It's like the train on a wedding dress!" She twirls across the floor until it falls out.

*

"Where should we look?" I ask Isabelle.

"Over there!" She points at Pet World and runs off.

I catch up to her in the store. "Isabelle, we can't buy our grandparents a puppy. That's on *your* list!"

After I drag her out of the store, we bump into my two best friends: Anthony Vernon and Xavier Bowen. When they hear I'm in charge of Isabelle, they feel sorry for me.

Then Anthony says, "So where is she?"

"Who?" I ask.

"Isabelle."

Oh no! I take one minute to talk to my friends and my sister disappears! That's a record, even for her.

"There she is!" says Xavier, in his high-pitched voice.

Isabelle appears out of nowhere. She's hopping towards us.

"My sister looks like a frog," I say.

"Or a kangaroo," adds Anthony.

"What about a grasshopper?" asks Xavier.

"Hi Anthony! Hi Xavier!" Isabelle hops up and greets them. "Have you seen my Christmas stocking?"

Uh-oh!

Isabelle's pointing at her feet. She's wearing a blue boot on her left foot and a red sock on her right.

"Isabelle! What did you do with your other boot?"

Her little thumb jerks towards the shoe store across the hall. I grab her wrist and take her over. My friends follow us.

"Where is it?" I ask when we get there.

"I'm not sure. It's in here somewhere," she says, opening her arms wide.

"Well that narrows it down," jokes Anthony. "How hard can it be to find a boot in a shoe store?"

Then he opens his arms wide, too. And points at aisle after aisle of boots that look exactly like my sister's.

The shoe store is having a sale right now: two boots for the price of one.

"I found it!" shouts Xavier. He waves a blue boot at us.

"Thanks so much, Xavier!" says Isabelle. "Can I have a kiss?" She grabs his scarf to pull him closer.

My sister is so annoying sometimes!

"Isabelle! Let go of him! His face is turning blue!"

"Hey! Xavier's turning into a Smurf!" says Anthony.

Isabelle lets go of the scarf and Xavier starts to breathe again.

We take a good look at the boot in his hands. It's the wrong one: Isabelle's name is not written in it. And it's for a left foot.

Xavier looks at his hands trying to remember which is the left.

Anthony decides to help him: "It's the hand you use — I mean, you don't use — to write. Unless you're left-handed. Then it is the hand you use to write."

"Thanks," says Xavier. Now he's pretending to write, trying to remember which hand he uses. "You just confused me even more!"

"You're welcome," Anthony says with a smile.

We decide we need help if we're going to find Isabelle's boot. Anthony goes off to look for a clerk. He comes back with a teenager with a thin moustache.

I've seen that moustache before. I think it was at the ski rental shop before I broke my ankle on a class field trip. But that's another story . . .

The sales clerk tells Isabelle to sit on the floor. She actually listens to him! Then he sits beside her, silently, with his eyes closed.

"What are you doing?" my sister asks.

"I'm going through the aisles in my mind."

"Can I go with you?" she asks, innocently.

"Thanks, but I'm . . . Oh, wait! I think I know where I saw it!"

He jumps up and walks to the end of an aisle. He picks up a blue boot.

I guess he knows more than just ski equipment.

He peeks inside the boot.

"Ta-dah!"

Xavier grabs it from him. He pretends to check that it's for the right foot. Then he reads out loud: "lebA ellebasI."

He pauses.

"What? 'Leba ellebasi?' That's not your sister's name," he says. "Maybe it's the country where the boots were made?"

I grab the boot. One look and I get it. "You're reading the name backwards, Xavier! 'Leba ellebasi' — that's Isabelle Abel the other way around."

"I knew that was my name!" shouts Isabelle. "I know everybody's name backwards. Like yours, Dominic, is ... um ... Leba Cinimod. Ha! Ha! Cinimod!"

Then she laughs wildly, bouncing up and down on her bum.

My sister is so strange sometimes!

"Let's get out of here, Cinimod!" Anthony says with a grin.

Isabelle bursts into laughter again.

We thank the clerk and leave the store.

Anthony and Xavier say they have to get going. I beg them to stay, but they start to walk away.

I promise to buy them each a large popcorn the next time we go to the movies. They accept the deal.

I bet Xavier wishes he had said no. Isabelle is hugging and kissing him non-stop.

Turning his face left and right, he manages to say, "Dominic . . . your . . . sister . . . is . . . soooo . . . Argh!"

He's too polite — or annoyed — to finish his sentence.

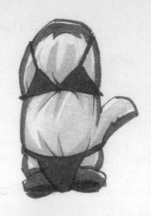

Chapter 3
The Missing Mitten

We decide we need to fuel up before we start shopping.

I buy a chocolate bar, some juice, chips and gummy bears. I had to buy the chocolate bar because Isabelle ate half of it while we were waiting in the lineup.

My sister is so much trouble sometimes!

As I hand my friends their food, I look down and realize Isabelle's gone again. It's the second time in half an hour. Another record, I'm sure!

Thirty seconds later, I spot her running towards me. Are those tears rolling down her cheeks?

"What happened, Isabelle?"

"I'm missing one of my mittens!"

She loves her mittens. Our grandma knitted them just for her.

"Oh, no. What now?" asks Xavier.

"My mitten!" she cries again.

"Poor little kitten has lost her mitten," sings Anthony.

"Where were you when you lost it?" I ask.

"In there." She points at a store.

This time she's pointing at a *lingerie* store! I can't go in there. I'll die of embarrassment!

"Why couldn't you have dropped it in a bookstore?" I ask.

"We have to help her," Anthony says. He looks kind of excited. "She must get her mitten back. Without it, her fingers could freeze and fall off!"

Isabelle turns to me in a flash. Her smile is so wide that I can see all her teeth. I hear her whisper the words, "Finger Fairy . . ."

I ignore her. I'm on a mission.

I pull my hat down to cover my forehead. I pull my scarf up to cover my nose. I am now "undercover."

A man's got to do, what a man's got to do!

"My mom doesn't want me to go in there," Xavier says. "I'll wait for you out here."

The rest of us go in. The mitten is probably on the floor, right? That's where a dropped mitten should end up.

So my plan is to keep my eyes down. But somehow they keep going up . . . to where the big posters are . . . the ones showing ladies in nightgowns.

I start to blush. But it's hard to look away. One of the poster ladies seems to be following me with her eyes. Just like the Mona Lisa. But in a bathing suit.

"I found my mitten!" shouts Isabelle.

Phew! "Where was it?"

"It was right there, Dominic. By that dressing room."

I look over without thinking. My legs get weak and shaky. The curtain isn't pulled closed all the way. I can see the back of a lady trying on a shirt or something . . . Her head is covered at first, then—

Oh, noooo! I have to get out of here! The lady in the dressing room is my teacher, Ms. Allison!

Chapter 4
What a Knockout

I run from the store with Isabelle and Anthony following me.

"What's wrong?" Xavier asks me.

Before I can answer him, we hear "Ho-ho-ho!" coming from Santa's Village.

"Let's go see Santa! I want to see Santa!" Isabelle shouts at the top of her lungs.

She takes off at a run.

My sister is so exhausting sometimes!

Wasting no time, my friends and I follow her.

She's a quick one. Even though she has short little legs, she stays ahead of us. Being small helps her cut through the crowd. She reminds me of a little mouse heading for a big piece of cheese.

When my friends and I reach Santa's Village, Isabelle is already standing in the lineup.

"Heeere, Dominic! Heeere!" Her arms are waving wildly in the air.

She's so excited, I can't be mad. I walk over to talk to her.

"So, what are you going to tell Santa you want for Christmas?" I ask.

"Well, I want . . ."

What follows is a long list of toys. Isabelle
has been studying store flyers for weeks.

"You can only tell Santa Claus one thing,"
I remind her.

She crosses her arms and starts to pout.

"It's not fair!" she whines.

My sister is so greedy sometimes!

The wait is very long.

Not far from Santa, I spot a tall Christmas tree. It has colourful cards and lights on it. It's the Joy-Giving Tree. I'll have to remind my parents to pick a kid's name from it again this year. Every Christmas my family buys a gift for a child in need. Then we get to turn on the light that matches the name we picked. My mom says it feels good to give joy.

"It's my turn!" Isabelle tells me.

Santa's elf takes her to The Big Chair. I drag my feet as I follow them.

Isabelle throws herself onto Santa's lap.
I see his mouth frown in pain behind his
white beard.

My friends are having a great time making fun of me. Anthony's bellowing, "Ho-ho-ho!" while Xavier sits on his lap, sucking his thumb. He's trying to get my sister to pull on Santa's beard. He really shouldn't do that!

"What would you like for Christmas, little girl?" Santa asks Isabelle.

"Well, Santa ... I'd really like an ... Xavier Bowen."

"Ho-ho— An Xavier Bowen?" Santa says, surprised. "What's an Xavier Bowen?"

Isabelle jerks her thumb in the direction of my friend.

"That's an Xavier Bowen. You can give him plenty of kisses. And when you pull on his scarf, his face turns blue!"

"Ho-ho-ho! Just like a Smurf! Well, I'll check and see if I have some left in my workshop. Do you want me to put him under your tree?" Santa asks.

"Oh, noooo — I want him in my Christmas stocking!"

To make my sister laugh, Santa switches hats with her. I didn't see that coming or I would have stopped him. We just heard about a lice outbreak in her class!

Santa switches the hats back. Isabelle jumps down from his lap. She's so happy, she starts hopping and bouncing everywhere.

Then Santa leans down to give her a kiss on the forehead. At the same time, she jumps up. Her head hits him in the chin!

Bang!

My sister is so hard-headed sometimes!

Santa falls to the ground. He's down for the count. He looks like a bearded ragdoll.

Isabelle is rubbing the top of her head. She looks hurt.

"Ow!" she cries.

Santa's elf is just standing there. He's staring at Santa with his mouth open, not moving.

Oh, wait! Yes, his shoulders are starting to shake. He hides his face in his hands. The elf is laughing!

Soon he's giggling so hard, he's almost falling over. Whenever it seems like he might calm down, he sees his boss and bursts into giggles again.

Anthony can't stand to be left out of the fun. He jumps on stage. He points one finger in Santa's direction and slowly moves it up and down. Then, in a loud voice, he starts: "1 . . . 2 . . . 3 . . . 4 . . . 5 . . ." He's pretending to be a referee at a boxing match!

Half the children in line are crying. A big crowd is starting to gather.

Santa's elf has fallen to the floor. He's pounding it with both fists. He's laughing so much that he's having a hard time breathing. His face is as red as Santa's suit!

"6 . . . 7 . . . 8 . . . 9 . . . 10!" Anthony grabs Isabelle's arm and lifts it in the air. Everyone's waiting for what he's going to say.

"The lightweight, Isabelle Abel, wins by a knockout over the heavyweight, Santa Claus. Thanks to a strong uppercut — I mean, head butt — thrown to the chin!"

Isabelle jumps up and down, like a boxer who's just won a fight. Anthony is grinning. He puts his hands on his hips and looks at Santa.

He bends down and says, "I can see why you prefer to *give* rather than *receive*. Ho-ho-ho! Merry Christmas!"

I look at all this and realize I was right. It was definitely a bad idea to bring Isabelle to the mall with me.

I'm happy to see that Santa is starting to move. People are trying to help him up.

My sister is so naughty sometimes!

Epilogue
Giving Joy

When we finally get home, I'm exhausted! As for Isabelle, she's still leaping around like a frog, or a kangaroo or a grasshopper. Too much chocolate, I think!

I had to stop her from making snow angels all the way home. And her boot fell off again. But *only* twice this time.

Xavier decided to give her a piggyback. She promised not to kiss him or pull his scarf!

My parents are happy to have us back. My dad ruffles my hair. I think he's proud of me.

My mom tries to calm Isabelle down so she can take off her snowsuit. Then she notices Anthony and Xavier. "I see you had some help buying the gifts, Dominic," she says.

The gifts? Oh, no! The gifts! I hit my forehead with the palm of my hand.

I was so busy taking care of Isabelle that I forgot why we went to the mall! We didn't get the presents for Grandma and Grandpa!

My parents seem to find this funny.

I'm sitting next to Isabelle, not quite sure why they're laughing. Anthony turns to our Christmas tree and picks out two large bows made of red and green ribbons. He sticks them on our heads.

"Why not give them Dominic and Isabelle as gifts?" asks Anthony. He seems proud of himself.

"I think we have some wrapping paper big enough!" answers my dad, with a twinkle in his eye.

My mom starts to laugh again. Xavier does, too. Anthony's holding his belly, imitating Santa's elf. My dad is bellowing, "Ho-ho-ho!"

I look at Isabelle. She's standing there, in front of our Christmas tree, with a big bow on her head. She has a wide smile on her face and she's batting her eyes.

My sister is so cute sometimes!

"Listen," says my mom. "Don't worry about the gifts. Dad and I will get them tomorrow."

I remind them to stop by the Joy-Giving Tree to pick a name.

"We'll do that, Dominic. It always feels good to—"

"—give joy. I know, Mom."

Isabelle is starting to jump up and down again.

"Yes! I want to go, too! Can I go with you?"

Now, that's a good idea! Hopefully I can stay home!

Alain M. Bergeron

An important point to note — my big sisters, Francine and Lise, were never on the Naughty List! Isabelle is not based on them at all. In fact, my sisters would probably identify more with our hero, Dominic. That's because they had to deal with two rowdy little brothers!

The Naughty List, Flying Low and *The Big Trip*, which feature Dominic and his friends, were all originally written in French.

My friend Sampar and I make a great team. We've worked on many other series together, including Savais-tu?, Petits pirates, Capitaine Static and Billy Stuart.

Thank goodness we like each other, too!

Sampar

Most of the time, I can illustrate books from the safety of my office. I travel in my imagination, or do research from books and the internet.

But sometimes an illustrator has to go out in the field to get the full picture. For *The Naughty List*, armed with nothing but my courage and a sketch pad, I went to the mall to check out a lingerie store! Wow. I really understood Dominic's reaction to all of the pictures of ladies in nighties. Their eyes really do seem to follow you everywhere!

It doesn't help that I tried to do a few sketches in the store. Of course, a sales clerk had to ask me what I was doing. Was I embarrassed? And how! That will teach me to illustrate books for my friend Alain!

Also in the series: